UG
AND THE
Cave Bear

by Sue Graves and Natalia Gubanova

W
FRANKLIN WATTS
LONDON•SYDNEY

Long ago in the Stone Age, there was
a boy called Ug. He lived in a deep cave
in the forest with his mum, dad
and little sister, Ika.

At the front of the cave was a fire.

The fire was very important. The family
cooked food on it. The fire kept them warm.
Most important of all, it kept them safe.
Wild animals, even bears, were scared
of the fire. Dad said it was important
that the fire never went out.

Every day, Ug and his dad looked for
wood and dry grass to put on the fire.
They stacked the wood and grass
in the cave until it was needed.

Dad and Mum were always looking for food to feed the family. Mum looked for nuts and berries, and Dad hunted for animals with the other men. He said it was safer to hunt in a group than to hunt alone.

Ug loved living in the cave. He liked painting pictures on its walls. He painted every day, using ash from the fire and juice that he squeezed from berries.

Mum said he was very clever.

One day, Dad said that he had seen
the footprints of a big animal in the forest.
He was going with his friends to hunt it.
There would be lots of meat for everyone.
Before they left, Dad and the other hunters
checked their spears were strong and sharp.

"I will pick nuts while Dad is hunting,"
Mum told Ug. "You must stay in the cave.
You must look after Ika, too."
"And remember – don't let the fire go out,"
said Dad.

Ug began painting a picture of
a mammoth hunt on the cave wall.

"Why are you painting that?" asked Ika.

"A picture of a mammoth hunt brings
good luck to the hunters," Ug told her.

"I want Dad to have good luck today."

Ika saw that the fire was nearly out.

"Ug, you must put more wood on the fire," she said.

"I'll do it soon," said Ug. "I must finish this picture first. It's important for the hunters."

A little later, Ika saw something moving by the trees. She thought it was Mum coming home. She looked out of the cave. A bear was coming closer and closer. "Ug, Ug!" she shouted. "A bear's coming. It's coming towards our cave!"

"Don't worry," said Ug, still painting.

"The fire will keep the bear away."

"But the fire has gone out!" yelled Ika.

13

Ug looked at where the fire should be.

He looked at the bear. He looked at his sister.

"Run!" he yelled.

Ug and Ika ran as fast as they could,

deep into the cave. They hid behind

the stack of wood and dry grass.

Ika was scared. She began to cry.

Ug had to think fast. "I must make fire," he said. "Fire will scare the bear away. Ika, quick, grab some of that dry grass!" Carefully, Ika poked the dry grass into the top of a big stick to make a fire stick. Ug grabbed some flint and struck it hard against the stone by the cave wall. "We've got to make the flint spark against the stone to set the grass on fire," said Ug.

Ug kept striking the flint against the stone,
just as he had seen Mum do.

"Hurry up!" shouted Ika. "The bear's coming!"

Ug's fingers began to sting, but he kept striking
the stone as hard as he could.

Suddenly, there were sparks, and the grass
set on fire.

Ug ran bravely towards the bear,

yelling loudly and waving his fire stick.

The bear turned and ran out of the cave

as fast as it could.

It ran right past Mum and Dad!

Ug told Mum and Dad what had happened.
He told them about his painting and why
the fire went out. He told them about
the cave bear and how he scared it away.
"You should have looked after the fire,"
said Dad. "I told you it was important.
Fire keeps us safe."

"I'm sorry," said Ug, sadly. "I will never let it go out again."

"Well, we need to make a new fire, Ug," said Dad. "Your picture of a mammoth hunt did bring us luck. We have plenty of meat. Let's get cooking!"

Story order

Look at these 5 pictures and captions.
Put the pictures in the right order
to retell the story.

1

Ug chased the bear with the fire stick.

2

Ika saw that the fire was out and a bear was coming.

3

Mum and Dad went out to look for food.

4

Ug drew a picture for the hunters.

5

Ug used flint to make a fire.

Independent Reading

This series is designed to provide an opportunity for your child to read on their own. These notes are written for you to help your child choose a book and to read it independently.
In school, your child's teacher will often be using reading books which have been banded to support the process of learning to read. Use the book band colour your child is reading in school to help you make a good choice. *Ug and the Cave Bear* is a good choice for children reading at White Band in their classroom to read independently. The aim of independent reading is to read this book with ease, so that your child enjoys the story and relates it to their own experiences.

About the book
This is a fictional story set during the time of the Stone Age. People at the time would have used fire to protect themselves from wild animals, and fire was often made by striking flint.

Before reading
Help your child to learn how to make good choices by asking: "Why did you choose this book? Why do you think you will enjoy it?" Ask your child what they know about the Stone Age. Explain that people living at the time usually ate what they could hunt and gather. Stone tools were used to help them hunt, and flint was used to make fire to warm and protect them. Look at the cover with your child and ask: "Where do you think the family live?" Remind your child that they can break words into groups of syllables or sound out letters to make a word if they get stuck. Decide together whether your child will read the story independently or read it aloud to you.

During reading
Remind your child of what they know and what they can do independently. If reading aloud, support your child if they hesitate or ask for help by telling them the word. If reading to themselves, remind your child that they can come and ask for your help if stuck.

After reading
Support comprehension by asking your child to tell you about the story. Use the story order puzzle to encourage your child to retell the story in the right sequence, in their own words.
The correct sequence can be found on the next page.
Help your child think about the messages in the book that go beyond the story and ask: "How do you think Ug felt when he saw that the fire had gone out?"
Give your child a chance to respond to the story: "Did you have a favourite part?"

Extending learning
Help your child predict other possible outcomes of the story by asking: "What do you think would have happened if Ug had not managed to make the fire?"
In the classroom, your child's teacher may be teaching comprehension skills, such as how the use of words and phrases can contribute to the meaning. Which words and phrases tell us that Ug suddenly understands there is an emergency? Find examples in the text, such as: '"Run!" he yelled', 'Ug had to think fast', '"Ika, quick, grab some of that dry grass!"', 'Ug grabbed some flint and struck it hard'.

Franklin Watts
First published in Great Britain in 2024
by Hodder and Stoughton
Copyright © Hodder and Stoughton, Ltd
All rights reserved.

Series Editors: Jackie Hamley and Melanie Palmer
Series Advisors and Development Editors: Dr Sue Bodman and Glen Franklin
Series Designers: Cathryn Gilbert and Peter Scoulding

A CIP catalogue record for this book is
available from the British Library.

ISBN 978 1 4451 8914 7 (hbk)
ISBN 978 1 4451 8915 4 (pbk)
ISBN 978 1 4451 9522 3 (ebook)

Printed in China

Franklin Watts
An imprint of
Hachette Children's Group
Part of Hodder and Stoughton
Carmelite House
50 Victoria Embankment
London EC4Y 0DZ

An Hachette UK Company
www.hachette.co.uk

www.reading-champion.co.uk

Answer to Story order: 3, 4, 2, 5, 1